Daddy All Day Long

Dedicated to my daddy, William Wright, and to the other special dads in my family:
Pat and Chuck Rusackas, Joel and Steven Wright.
—F.R.

With much love, respect, and gratitude for my very own wonderful daddy, Ruben Garcia,
my terrific dad-in-law, Omer Burris, and my children's own incredible dad, Craig.
And to Ellen Sussman, forever thankful for you;
to Stephanie and Judy, always your loyal and humble fan.
—P.B.

Daddy All Day Long
Text copyright © 2004 by Francesca Rusackas
Illustrations copyright © 2004 by Priscilla Burris

Manufactured in China by South China Printing Company Ltd.
All rights reserved.
www.harperchildrens.com
Francesca Rusackas's website is www.kiddzone.com

Library of Congress Cataloging-in-Publication Data
Rusackas, Francesca.
Daddy all day long / by Francesca Rusackas ; illustrated by Priscilla Burris. — 1st ed.
p.   cm.
Summary: Owen pig and his daddy count the ways they love each other from one to ten and a million zillion more all day long.
ISBN 0-06-050284-3 — ISBN 0-06-050285-1 (lib. bdg.)
[1. Fathers and sons—Fiction. 2. Love—Fiction. 3. Bedtime—Fiction. 4. Pigs—Fiction. 5. Counting.]
I. Burris, Priscilla, ill. II. Title.
PZ7.R892Dad 2004
2003007013 [E]—dc21 CIP AC
Typography by Adriana Cordero
1   2   3   4   5   6   7   8   9   10
❖
First Edition

Daddy All Day Long

by Francesca Rusackas
illustrated by Priscilla Burris

HarperCollins*Publishers*

Owen had something special to tell his daddy.

"Daddy," said Owen,
"I love you more than chocolate milk!"

"Chocolate milk?" said Daddy.
"Well, I love you more than
    TWO pancakes with bananas on top!"

"Your pancakes are yummy, but I love you more than THREE piggyback rides!"

"Then I love you more than FOUR trips down the slide!" said Daddy.

"Well, I love you more than
SIX monster tickles!" said Daddy.

Owen ran into their house and plopped onto his chair.

"I love you more than SEVEN scoops
of ooey-gooey chocolate caramel ice cream!"

"I love you more than NINE bedtime stories."

"I love you, my little Owen, more than TEN giant hugs!"

"Hugs are good, but I love you
more than ONE HUNDRED fireflies!"

"That's a lot of stars!
But I love you more than
ONE MILLION ZILLION kisses!"